How to Survive a Totally Boring Summer

ALSO BY ALICE DELACROIX

Mattie's Whisper

The Hero of Third Grade

HOW TO Survive A Totally Boring Summer

ALICE DELACROIX

iLLUSTRaTed by CYNTHIA FISHER

Holiday House / New York

Library of Congress Cataloging-in-Publication Data

DeLaCroix, Alice.
How to survive a totally boring summer / by Alice DeLaCroix ; illustrated by
Cynthia Fisher.—1st ed.
p. cm.
Summary: When Randall and his friend Max start a chess club in the park
to keep busy during the summer, there are unexpected benefits for the
community.
ISBN-13: 978-0-8234-2024-7 (hardcover)
[1. Chess—Fiction.   2. Clubs—Fiction.   3. Community life—Fiction.
4. Interpersonal relations—Fiction.]   I. Fisher, Cynthia, ill.   II. Title.
PZ7.D36965How 2007
[Fic]—dc22
2006024891

For my wonderful critique group:
MJ Auch, Marsha Hayles,
Jennifer Meagher, and Vivian VandeVelde
They are never boring

Contents

How to Survive a Totally Boring Summer

Chapter 1
Opening Moves

"She's going to crash!"

"Oh, no! Come on, Max!" said Randall. He and his new best friend, Max, had been sitting under the huge beech tree between their apartment buildings. It was their meeting place.

"Tara!" Randall yelled as they ran to the sidewalk. The girl on Rollerblades lurched closer. Her arms flailed, so she looked like a bird. Her steps chop-chopped.

"We'll save you," Randall said.

Tara came to a jolting stop. "No you won't. I can stop just fine!"

Max smiled, which made his ears go up.

Randall said with a smile of his own,

"Looks like you can stop better than you can go."

Tara shrugged. "Your sidewalks are rough. Anyway, I made it all the way here from my house. What are you guys up to?" she asked with her usual piercing need to know.

"Not much," said Max.

"We're trying to figure out what to do this summer. What goes on around here?" Randall asked. He'd lived in Rushport only about three months. This would be his first school vacation in a new place. It had better not drag. And besides, he was worried nothing could be as much fun as summers had been back home.

Max and Tara answered together, "Not much." Tara made a face.

Ugh, and double ugh! Randall thought. He liked to keep busy. Suddenly he grabbed Max's arm, because he saw someone peeking around the corner of the building. Someone big. Someone whose middle name was Trouble.

"I think Gordo is snooping on us," he said.

"We should just ignore him," Max said softly.

Tara had other ideas. "Oh, that pain!" she said. "Gordo, get over here. Now! We see you. "

Maybe Gordo wasn't so brave when he didn't have any of his buddies with him. He didn't come. He disappeared.

"Arrgh! If I didn't have these things on my feet, I'd chase him," said Tara.

Randall figured she would, too. He said, "Forget it." But Tara was right—Gordo was a pain. He had given Randall a hard time at school. In fact, he gave lots of the third grade class trouble. No, Randall wasn't happy to learn that Gordo might be part of his summer.

"Swimming," Max said.

"Huh?"

"I'm taking swim lessons this summer."

"I've had swim lessons," said Randall. "Every summer since I was five, I think."

Tara held her nose and pretended to sink under water. "Glub, glub," she said, making the boys laugh.

"I've had them, too," Max went on. "But we can take diving this year."

"Diving? Great," Randall said. "I'll ask if I can." He knew they didn't have much extra money now that he and his mother were living apart from Dad. But swim lessons might be cheap.

Now Tara was making swimming motions with her arms.

"Hey, Tara, how about you?" Max said.

"Dunno. Maybe. You guys should do the summer reading program, too."

"Oh, right," said Max. "I did that last summer. You get the books at the library, so it's free."

Mom would like that and so would he, Randall decided, and nodded. Still, it was going to take more than swim classes and reading to fill his time. He needed a project. One that didn't include Gordo, for sure.

Just then a window was opened on the second floor of Randall's apartment building.

Mrs. Mickovitch stuck her head out. "Randall!" she called. "Lunch is ready."

Mrs. Mick was Randall's next-door neighbor. She was looking after him for the vacation weeks while his mother worked at the bank. All except the week he would spend with his dad.

"Bring your friends," she said. "I've made krupnick." She shut the window without waiting for an answer.

"Want to come?" Randall asked.

Tara said, "Krup for lunch? Uh-uh! See you later." She took off, arms pumping.

"I'm in," Max said, "but I'll have to call my mom to let her know."

Mrs. Mick met them at her door. Randall's mother had said Mrs. Mickovitch was seventy–two. But she was still tall and straight, and wore her silver hair in a pony-tail. "Good, good," she said, seeing that Max had come along. "I raised three boys of my own, so I like a crowd."

Randall didn't think two was much of a crowd, but he smiled.

"Love ya, gorgeous," said a coarse voice.

6

"Huh?" said Max.

Randall laughed. "Don't freak. It's just Romeo, Mrs. Mick's parrot. He says that a lot."

"Love ya, gorgeous." The green parrot strutted sideways across the back of a chair. It was where he liked to be when not in his cage.

"Wow, he's big. And really green," Max said.

"And look at that big yellow beak," Randall said.

"He's some bird, for sure." Then Max remembered to ask if he could use the phone.

At the kitchen table eating his krupnick (which turned out to be a Polish barley, beef, and vegetable soup), Randall thought more about this summer. He bet everybody had neat things they'd be doing. He didn't want to feel left out. He asked Max, "I don't suppose you play chess, do you?"

Max's eyes widened. "Sure I do. It's the best."

Randall grinned. He couldn't get over how many ways he liked Max.

"My dad taught me how," he said. "He even made me a chessboard." Randall's throat could still close up on him when he talked about his dad. But chess with him had been fun, so he was able to swallow his next mouthful of soup.

Mrs. Mick said, "Oh my, I remember chess when I was growing up. Wonderful game! But I've never seen kids play it here, dumpling."

Randall winced. He wasn't used to being called dumpling. But Mom said Mrs. Mick had come from Poland, and Polish dumplings were good food.

He told her, "Lots of kids play. At least they did where I lived before. There was even a chess club for kids."

Max looked at Randall with his eyebrows *and* his ears raised.

Randall thought a second, then said, "Yeah!" Now he knew what he wanted for his project. He and Max could start a chess club!

Couldn't they?

Chapter 2
Plans and Strategy

"And there are tables right in the town park, and that's what they're made for, to play chess on. So the club can meet there."

Randall had been telling Mom his chess club idea at supper that evening. "Max and I think two times a week would be okay. What do you think, Mom?"

"Chess club is a great idea, honey." She fiddled with her fork. "But the park is several blocks away. And there wouldn't be an adult with you."

"Mom, I'm not a baby. Max and I can walk over together. And Mrs. Mick could check on us—if she has to—and some of the kids will probably need to be brought, so their parents won't be far off, I bet."

Mom was nodding.

"Anyway, this is a really small town. The park is friendly, don't you think?"

"Well, yes, it seems to be. It's a lovely park with all those flowers, and the swings and the benches. I like that it's a kind of old-fashioned town square with the town hall and shops and the library all around it."

"Uh-huh, and that reminds me—Tara and Max are signing up for a summer reading program at the library. I could do that, too, and we'd be able to pick out new books after chess some days."

Mom grinned. "Well, I'm impressed, honey. Okay, I agree to your club *and* to the library reading program. Just let me be sure Mrs. Mick doesn't mind. In case she does need to be there."

"All right! Mrs. Mick won't care. She's got lots of energy." In Mrs. Mick's apartment Randall had seen some old photos of her doing high kicks in a chorus line. He wouldn't be surprised if she still could do them.

"Now, how about some of that dessert in the fridge?" Mom said.

"All right! Chocolate pudding!"

Mom smiled. "You serve, okay?"

Randall spooned pudding into two bowls. He sat and slurped smooth pudding between his teeth, even though his mother frowned at him. It was just so good, and he was feeling happy.

Mom picked up a blue sheet of paper from the small cart beside the table. It was all she had as a desk now in this new apartment. "I'd like you to take swim lessons, too. It wouldn't be summer without them, would it?"

"Nope, it wouldn't. Max and I want to be in the same class. I was going to ask you about that next—after dessert."

Over the phone his mother and Max's made plans for the swim lessons. Mrs. Johnson was happy to take Randall to the high school pool and back so the boys could be together. The first class was in two days.

Randall wished it would be that simple to make chess club happen. Now that he had permission, he wasn't sure how to get things going. How many kids? How to get them to come? Should he put up posters? So many questions. But hey, it was a *project*, wasn't it?

And by the first swim class, Randall had a plan for chess club.

On the way home from the pool, Mrs. Johnson dropped the boys off at the town park. "We need to check things out," Randall had told Max earlier.

Mrs. Johnson said, "Remember, I want you home in an hour."

Max tapped his watch. "We can time the walk home," he told Randall. "That way we'll know for sure how long it will take to get here for club meetings."

"Yeah," Randall agreed. Max was a good partner. Randall didn't even have a watch. "What time is it now?"

"Ten thirty-five."

The park wasn't big; you could see across it. Nothing about Rushport was very big. There was only one main street and a few side streets. The main street split in the middle where the town square park was, then went back together on the other side. Randall liked Rushport. He thought he could get to know it before too long. And maybe it would get to know him, so he wouldn't feel strange.

Randall made a beeline for the small tables near the center of the park. "All right!" he said, slapping the cement table top. "All four tables are empty!"

"So, morning will be a good time for us to meet?"

"Looks like it," Randall said.

"What makes you think they're empty every morning?" asked a gruff voice.

Randall started. He hadn't even noticed the old man sitting on a park bench. The bench was gray; he was gray. He was bent over, tossing food to a gang of pigeons, also gray. The pigeons acted tame around him.

"Well," Randall said, "our chess club would just need them a couple mornings a week. Like from ten till eleven o'clock. Is that possible?"

"Maybe. Maybe not." The man folded his paper bag of birdseed and slowly stood to quite a height. "Hmpf, chess club," he said with a sneer. Then without another word he shuffled off. One of the pigeons flew to his shoulder and rode there a ways.

Randall and Max looked at each other. "What a grouch," said Max.

"Yeah. Guess he doesn't like kids. I can't believe the birds like *him*," said Randall.

"Birdman." He rolled his eyes. "Anyhow, do you think there is someone we need to ask about the tables?"

Max shook his head. "It's like a bench, or a swing. You are allowed to use it if no one else has it."

"That makes sense," Randall said. "So if we have swimming Monday, Wednesday, and Friday . . ."

"Tuesday and Thursday can be chess club," Max finished for him.

"Now all we need are people!"

"Yep, club members," agreed Max.

Okay, so he didn't have a *perfect* plan yet. "We'll figure it out," he said.

"Sure. Let's go over to the library now and get signed up. Then we can start timing our walk home."

Randall gave a satisfied nod and one last look at the four chess tables.

After the library, the walk home from the park took twelve minutes and thirteen seconds. That's what Max's watch showed.

Randall hurried on to Mrs. Mick's.

Chapter 3
Wrong Move

Swimming had made Randall even hungrier than usual for lunch. He wondered what good Polish food Mrs. Mick would have for him today.

But the second she answered the door, Mrs. Mick said, "Finally you're here!" She pulled Randall into the living room. "Now you can help me."

"Okay," Randall said, not sure what was going on. His stomach growled loudly, but Mrs. Mick didn't seem to notice. She was frowny. Strands of hair dangled in her face, loose from her ponytail.

"What should I . . ." he started to ask, when Mrs. Mick dropped to her hands and knees and peered under the sofa. When she stood up, her face was red.

"I've looked there two times already," she said. She dashed to the window, grabbed the long draperies, and shook them. "Come out, come out you old villain, you."

Suddenly Randall realized he hadn't been greeted by a "Love ya, gorgeous" when he'd come in. "Ohmygosh! Where's Romeo?"

Mrs. Mick glared at Randall. "If I knew the answer to that, do you think I'd be crawling around on the floor?"

"You don't know where he is?" Randall held his breath.

"No, no, NO! Don't know!" Mrs. Mick collapsed into her easy chair.

"Golly," said Randall. "I'm sorry you're upset. Maybe he—"

"Upset? I'm wild. I'm crazy! Where can my Romeo be?"

"I'll help you find him, Mrs. Mick." Romeo was a large bird. Randall wasn't sure he would even fit under a sofa.

Mrs. Mick sniffed and drew herself up. "Of course you'll help me. I've been waiting for you," she said crisply.

Randall didn't really know what to do. He'd never seen Mrs. Mick like this. "Okay," said Randall, hoping he *could* help her. "Has Romeo been out of his cage all morning?" He saw the cage door was still open.

She nodded.

"Well," he said, trying to think like a detective. It didn't come naturally. "Well," he repeated. "Did you leave the apartment?"

"No, I was here. Housecleaning."

"Have you searched every room?"

"Yes, quickly, but I just missed him a few minutes ago and only started looking then. I can't find him anywhere." Her frown deepened.

Randall opened a closet door to see if Romeo might have gotten into there. It was stuffed with old-smelling coats, hatboxes, and untidy piles of gloves and scarves on the high shelf, but no parrot.

Mrs. Mick watched him, her arms folded across her chest.

"Has he ever *hidden* before? Maybe he's playing a game. He's a mighty smart bird."

"Oh, he is that. Could be he sneaked out of one room as I went into another."

Randall said, "I'll go into the bedroom, and you stay in the living room."

Mrs. Mick cried, "Wait! Ohhh!" and dashed to the kitchen. Randall followed.

"Now look what's happened." Soup was bubbling up like a small volcano, over the pan edge onto the stove. Randall wrinkled his nose at the smell. "I forgot about lunch!" She turned off the burner and moved the pan to a cool spot. "Go, go." Mrs. Mick shooed him back out. "Look in the bedroom."

Randall opened the bedroom door and peeked in. No Romeo to be seen.

"Well, go on," said Mrs. Mick from the living room. "I was cleaning in there last."

Randall did a quick look-over. If Romeo was in the bedroom, he was well hidden. The bird did like high places. Was he on the curtain rod? It should be easy to spot a two-foot-high bright green bird.

"Ah-ha!" said Randall. "Mrs. Mick, can you come here?"

"Look," he pointed when she came into the room. "That window is wide open."

Mrs. Mick's chin dropped. "Oh, no. Oh, no, no, no!"

But Randall was nodding yes. He said, "I bet Romeo flew out while you weren't looking."

"That rascal!" she said. "I was shaking my dust mop. I can't believe I forgot to close the window!"

"Golly," said Randall. Romeo gone! Poor Mrs. Mick.

But Mrs. Mickovitch was perking up. "Well, I'll leave it open. He'll come back. He'll fly right back home. I know my Romeo."

"So he's flown away before?"

"No, never!" She set her face firmly. "I just know."

Randall hoped she was right. That woman was sure attached to her beautiful parrot. Maybe it was all those "Love ya, gorgeous" greetings she got. But he worried for her, anyway.

Chapter 4
Setting up

"Love ya, gorgeous!"

"He's back!" Randall had been with Mrs. Mick last evening until his mother came for him after work. At that time Romeo was still missing. Mom had wanted to help find the parrot somehow, but Mrs. Mick had convinced her to go on home.

Now Mrs. Mick was practically dancing. "Didn't I tell you he would come home?"

"When? How?" asked Randall as he circled Romeo's hanging cage. And why hadn't Mrs. Mick called to let him know Romeo was back safe? He'd had some trouble getting to sleep last night because of Romeo. He didn't like anyone to lose someone they loved, and Mrs. Mick loved this bird.

"Well, I left the window open and the bedroom door open, and about halfway through my game show, here he was." She held a treat through the cage wires. "You didn't bother to say where you'd gone, though, did you, Romeo, love?" she added.

"Is he okay?"

"Good as gold," Mrs. Mick said. "In fact, he's full of spunk. Maybe he needs to get out once in a while."

"But you might really lose him," said Randall.

"You know, it just doesn't feel that way to me. Now that he's been out and returned . . . hmmm . . . I don't know, I'll have to give it some thought."

"It was scary, though, when he was gone."

Mrs. Mick smoothed her hair back. "A little, I suppose."

Randall looked at her. What? Didn't she remember being wild? Crazy? Huh?

"Sometimes a little spreading of wings is good for the soul." She studied the parrot a moment. "Well, as I say, I'll have to think about it. Now, Randall, what do you have in mind for today?"

Randall drew a folded paper from the pocket of his shorts. "Phone calls. I want to call kids I know to see if they'll be in the chess club. This list has the names of every-one in my third grade class."

"Do you have the phone numbers?"

"Yep." He pointed as Mrs. Mick looked over his shoulder. "I'm going to call Walker, Jenna, and Dylan. And Max will call Tara and Caitlin." Last night, he and Max had decided chess club would be most fun with friends from their school class.

Now Randall reached for the phone. But his hand stopped in midair. Maybe he and Max were the only ones who thought chess was the best. Or maybe no one would want to be in a club that he had dreamed up.

"What's the matter, dumpling?"

"What if no one wants to be in my chess club?"

Mrs. Mick looked him in the eye. "If not, you can handle it, Randall. But my advice is, think positive. Oh, yes, and the only people who fail are the ones who never try. That's a good one, too, don't you think?"

Randall had to chuckle.

"Why, when I was a dancer in shows, I had to go to tryouts over and over. And that's how I got to be in many wonderful musicals," Mrs. Mick said. "You have to try!"

So Randall punched in Walker's number and started making calls.

"Love ya, gorgeous" rang out several times while he was talking on the phone. It helped Randall keep up his positive feeling.

After lunch Randall met Max under their tree.

"That was easy-peasy," said Randall. "Walker wants to join the club, and so does Jenna. They don't really know how to play, but that's okay. That's part of the reason for being in a club." He tossed a small red ball from hand to hand as he talked. Then he lobbed it to Max.

"Caitlin said yes, too," Max said. "But Tara wasn't home, so I'll have to try . . ."

"No you won't. Here she comes right now," said Randall. He took off to meet Tara as she whizzed along on her Rollerblades.

"Hey, you're getting good on those things," Randall told Tara.

Tara grinned. "What did you expect? Natural talent. And practice."

Max smiled. He asked her about joining the chess club.

"Sounds good. Who else is in it? Not Gordo, I hope," Tara said.

Randall frowned. "Not Gordo, for sure."

"He tried to trip me on the way over here."

Max looked around. "Did he follow you here again?"

"Uh-uh. He lives on my block, but I told him to get lost."

"That Gordo," Randall said, shaking his head.

Tara rolled her eyes.

Randall told Tara which kids had agreed to be in the chess club. "And if you and Caitlin can come up with one more person, we'll have an even number."

"Can do," Tara said.

The three of them tossed the ball back and forth, but Tara didn't want to take her skates off, so soon she zoomed away again.

"You know what?" Randall said. "Our club needs a name."

"Hey, yeah. A neat name," Max agreed.

Randall said, "How about . . . How about the Chess Set?"

Max blew a raspberry.

"Yeah, that stinks." He plopped down and pulled some blades of grass, thinking.

"Could we name it something that's not *club*? *Club* sounds like grown-ups," said Max.

"Something more like sports, maybe," Randall said. "Uh, team ... No, I got it! *Squad.*"

"Hey, I like it. Chess Squad."

They looked at each other, frowning. "I know ... I got it! Checkmate. The Checkmate Squad," said Randall.

Max said, "That's it!"

"Now as long as the parents say it's okay, we'll be all set."

Max tossed the ball back to Randall. "I hope they say yes."

"Think positive." Randall threw the ball high. "Yay, Checkmate Squad!"

Chapter 5
Forced into a Corner

On Tuesday, Randall woke with a start. Today was the day! First meeting of the Checkmate Squad. How could he wait until time to head to the park? But hold on, what would he do if the chess tables were taken? He'd be such a loser. He should have checked at the library to see if his club could meet there as well. Some days it might be raining. What a dope he was.

But when he and Max got to the park, Randall breathed a sigh of relief. "Whew! I was scared the tables would be taken," he confessed.

"Me, too, a little," agreed Max.

Randall put the box that held his chess

pieces on one table. It felt good to be setting up for play. It had been awhile.

"Hey, Randall!" It was Jenna calling as she walked near. Caitlin was with her. And a lady.

Randall and Max waved as Caitlin turned to the lady. "You can go on to the library, Mom. They're here already."

"I didn't bring anything, Randall," said Jenna with a flip of her ponytail. "That's okay, isn't it? You didn't say bring stuff."

"Sure, it's okay." As Max started setting out his chess pieces Randall said, "Tara has a set, and Dylan does too. We'll have enough for four tables to play."

"Cool," she said, picking up a chess piece. "A horse! I love horses."

Randall said, "It looks like a horse, but it's called a knight."

"Ooh, I love knights," said Jenna, "and knights rode horses."

Just then Randall noticed the tall gray man take a seat on the park bench nearest the tables. *Birdman*, Randall thought. At least he still hoped they'd get to use all four tables today. The man began feeding the gathering pigeons.

Jenna was saying, "I've never played chess, you know that, don't you? Tara said I'd learn."

Randall said, "Yep. We'll teach you. Some of us have played; some haven't."

"Are you any good at teaching?" asked Caitlin.

"Well—oh, here come the others." Gulp. Would he be any good? He'd thought about it the last few days and tried to remember things his dad had said early on. The basic steps weren't that hard to pick up. But he knew you could learn more and more about playing the longer you spent at it. It could take years and years to be really good. He liked that about the game.

Anyway, he was sure Caitlin would let him know if he made any mistakes.

"Hi, you guys," said Tara. "Meet Rosie. She's my neighbor, and she wants to be in the club." Tara pulled the small, shyly smiling girl around in front of her.

Randall said hi and so did Max, but he had thought Tara would bring someone from their own class.

"Rosie's going to be in third grade. But she's been playing chess since she was five," Tara explained.

Rosie's smile widened, but she still hadn't made a peep.

"So, everyone's here," said Max.

"Yeah, let's get started," Randall said. "Let's pair up—one who knows the rules with one who doesn't at each table."

All at once Birdman moved to one of the chess tables. He sat down. He laid a velvet bag on the table and began slowly pulling chess pieces from it. Beautiful, glasslike chess pieces.

Randall and Max stared. Max's mouth hung open. This wasn't how they'd planned it. Not at all.

"Randallll," Caitlin whined. "He's taking one of our tables. Do something."

What in the world could he say to an old man? Especially a big, grouchy one. But everyone was waiting for Randall. He

swallowed hard and then edged over to him. "Uh, mister—"

"What?" It was hardly a word. More like a snap. He continued setting up the board.

"Uh, we are a chess club. This is our first-ever meeting. We have enough people to use

all four of the tables. Since you don't have an
opponent, well, would you mind if—"

"This table was free when I sat down.
Now I have it." Birdman peered at him from
under feathery gray brows.

Randall knew he'd been dismissed, but

he couldn't give up. "But you can't play alone, so—"

"Excuse me, young fella," said a second old man, who had slipped up behind Randall. And to Birdman he said, "May I join you in a game?"

"Certainly." Birdman motioned for the second man to sit.

"This is fine. Fine, indeed. Wherever there is a chess game, that's the place for me. I'm Harold, by the way."

Jenna piped up, "It's okay, Randall. I can watch."

"Yeah, me, too." Tara made a little face.

Randall could tell Tara would rather play. He chewed his lip. He'd failed his club kids already.

Max shrugged. He said, "So Rosie plays with Walker, Randall with Caitlin, and me with Dylan."

Randall nodded. It wasn't total disaster. "Sometimes a game goes fast," he said, "and we can change players so that Jenna and Tara play next."

But Randall still seethed at Birdman. It seemed deliberate that he was here at this time. With his chessmen. And it seemed mean.

Chapter 6
INTO BATTLE

Randall sat down across from Caitlin. She was looking pleased with herself.

"Hold on, " said Randall. "You've changed the pieces around. They have to start on the squares where I had them."

Caitlin blinked. "Why?"

"Because the black queen always starts on a dark square . . . and every piece starts in a certain place."

"Why?"

Urrgh! Randall thought. This was going to be a trial. "Because that's the rule."

Caitlin did like rules. "Okay." She reset the two pieces she had moved.

Jenna stood at their table to watch. "How do you win this game? Most points?"

"You win when you could take your opponent's king in your next move, and there is nowhere he can move to prevent it. That's called checkmate." Randall looked at Caitlin and Jenna, then went on. "First, though, you have to know what each piece is named—"

"Yeah, like Brittney, or Ben," Jenna said, and giggled.

Randall smirked. "You're joking, aren't you?"

Caitlin held up a piece. "I know this is the queen," she said.

"Right."

"Well, you already said this was a knight. And I think this piece has to be king," said Jenna. "It looks like it."

"Right again." Then Randall showed her the rooks, bishops, and pawns. "Each piece is able to move only in a certain way. The pawns move one square at a time, and forward. Except when they capture a piece—"

"Aah, capture," said Caitlin, her eyes gleaming.

"Yeah, then they move one square diagonally." He carefully explained the movements for the other pieces.

"I start," said Randall.

Caitlin asked, "Why?"

"White always starts. That's the rule." It had worked before.

Caitlin's eyes were cool now. "But I wonder, why are you starter? Why not me? That would be better manners."

Randall sighed. "Only while you learn, okay?"

Caitlin checked out the other tables to see if the "teachers" were making their "beginners" do the same. "Go ahead, Randall," she said then.

He made his opening move and explained to Caitlin and Jenna why he'd opened that way. When they finally had the game going along and Caitlin was busy thinking, Randall looked around at the others. Every eye seemed glued to the chess tables. It was going okay!

Birdman and his opponent were mostly silent, planning their next moves.

Randall knew that's what it took to really play.

He heard Max say, "Oops, you don't want to move your queen out so early. She's too valuable."

Dylan chanted, "Rook, rookie, rookie, what do I want to do with my rookie?"

Then Caitlin brought Randall back. "I don't get it," she said. "If knights can jump, why can't the bishops?"

"Because that's the—"

"Rule! I know, I know," Caitlin said.

"Lots of rules to this game," said Jenna. She twisted her beaded bracelet.

"Yeah, but you'll get them. We've got all summer. See, this is like two armies. And you'd never be able to figure out moves to win if the pieces were allowed to move any which way. You just have to remember which ones move which way, then you can plan captures and how to trap the king. Like this," Randall said, and took one of Caitlin's pawns.

Next time Randall looked up from the board, he gulped. Gordo. Gordo was walking by. And turning and coming back again.

Randall thought, Go away! Go away!

But Gordo kept coming. His untied shoe-strings flapped. He popped a large glob of bubblegum. He angled closer to the tables. Oh, no! Just when things were shaping up.

He budged right in next to Randall and Caitlin's table.

Jenna, across from him, scowled. "You're not part of the club," she said.

Then Tara saw him, too. "Gordo, what are you doing here?" she demanded.

"It's a public park, isn't it? I can be here if I want." He pretend-tripped into the table and slapped his hand down as if to steady himself. Pieces scattered. "Oops, sorry," he said, but then he laughed.

Sorry? Yeah, right, thought Randall. Randall ground his teeth. Now he and Caitlin would have to start their game all over!

He wished he were brave enough to make Gordo go away. But he ducked his head and reset chess pieces instead.

Gordo clomped to another table. Randall heard Tara say, "Keep your big mitts off, Gordo."

Gordo snorted. "Am I hurting anything? Am I?" he asked all innocent-like. He moved on to Max's table and stayed there watching. Popping gum, slouching. But watching.

At least he was quiet for once.

Chapter 7
Sacrifice

Gordo hadn't ruined any other games. He had watched, then pulled Jenna's ponytail and trotted off before the hour was up. So Randall tried to think of Gordo the way Max did—if he ignored him, maybe he'd disappear.

Max and Randall got back to the apartment complex almost without realizing it. On the walk home they had gone over every little thing about the first meeting.

"Only a day and a half and it'll be Checkmate Squad time again," said Max.

"Can't wait!" Randall said as they got to Max's building. "See you in the morning for diving class."

Randall strode into Mrs. Mick's apartment. "What do ya say, Romeo?" He tapped the parrot's cage.

"Love ya, gorgeous!"

Randall laughed. "Yeah, that's what you say, for sure."

Mrs. Mick asked, "So, dumpling, how was the Checkmate Squad?"

Randall liked that she remembered his club name. "Great! Everybody showed up— can you believe it?—every last body. And they all acted really interested."

Mrs. Mick took him by the hands and twirled him around with her. "I knew it. You are one clever boy, Randall."

Randall grinned. "It'll be a good club, I think. If all the kids learn the rules, we'll have fun with winner playing winner." He scratched his head. "If everyone keeps on coming. And really tries." As usual, he was having some self-doubts. He plopped on the sofa, frowning. "And we only had three of the four tables. That slowed us down."

Mrs. Mick raised her eyebrows and waited.

Randall twisted his mouth. "There's this grouchy gray man at the park. I call him Birdman because he feeds the birds. And they hang around him like he's the Tasty-Freeze truck. Well, he brought his chess stuff and took a table before we could get it."

Mrs. Mick waited for more.

"I know, anyone can use them. But he heard me and Max planning our times for the Checkmate Squad to meet. It just didn't seem fair."

"Well, you managed, didn't you? Probably he won't be there next meeting."

Randall didn't want to talk anymore about it. He just hoped Mrs. Mick was right.

And he double-hoped that Gordo wouldn't be there again. He wasn't even going to mention him to Mrs. Mick. Nope, ignore Gordo, that was the idea.

The next morning Mom gave him a hug when she left him with Mrs. Mick. He set his swim bag and his library book down, then said hi to Romeo.

"He's not very chatty this morning," Mrs. Mick said. "Why don't you let him out of his cage? He'll thank you for it."

Randall unlatched the cage door, and Romeo flew to perch on the chair back. He turned his head this way and that. His little yellow eyes watched as Randall held out a fruity treat to him.

"Good bird, Romeo," Randall said when he took it in his curved beak.

"Love ya, gorgeous, " said Romeo.

Mrs. Mick chuckled. "See? He likes his freedom."

"And his treat," said Randall.

A little later Randall met Max and Mrs. Anderson outside to go to swimming class.

"Randall! Dumpling!" Mrs. Mick called down to him.

Yikes! Did she have to call him dumpling in public? Randall looked up and saw she was leaning out the window. "What?" he said.

"I'm making krupnick again, so maybe your friend Max will join us for lunch. Okay?"

Before he or Max could answer, Romeo escaped out the open window, his green wings pumping strongly.

"Ohh!" said Mrs. Mick. She was surprised, but then she said, "Look at him go!"

"Oh, no!" Randall said. "Romeo, come back here!" But the bird flew fast and around the corner. "Birds don't listen," said Randall.

"Come on," Max said, and started running. He and Randall darted down the sidewalk, turned the corner, looked up and down.

No bird.

"I thought he came this way," said Max.

"Yeah, he did."

Randall peered into the branches of a tree.

No parrot. No Romeo anywhere.

"Where could he have gotten to?" said Max.

"He's lost for sure this time," said Randall.

Max's mother caught up to them. "Mrs. Mickovitch says she'll leave her window open. Not to worry. Let him spread his wings, she says." She shook her head.

Randall explained about Romeo's last escape. "Mrs. Mick thinks a little spreading of wings is good for you."

"Oh, dear," said Mrs. Anderson. "That's a valuable parrot, I imagine."

"Yeah," said Randall, worried again. Especially valuable since Mrs. Mick loved him.

And sure enough, when Randall and Max got back to Mrs. Mick's for lunch, Romeo was still gone.

It was a quiet lunch. Clouds seemed to gather around the table with each one of Mrs. Mick's sighs.

Randall wanted to tell her it would be okay, because Romeo came back last time. But he wasn't so sure.

He hurried and finished his soup. "Come on, Max. We'll go back out and look for Romeo again."

Rumble . . . rumble! BOOM!

Randall jumped. Max jerked. Mrs. Mick cried, "Heavens!"

They all rushed to the living room window. Clouds had gathered—*real* ones. Big, dark, rolling clouds. *ZING!*

"Whoa, did you see that?" Randall's eyes were big.

"Lightning," said Max.

"Thunder, lightning—uh-oh, here comes the rain," said Mrs. Mick.

And it poured.

Mrs. Mick wrung her hands as the three of them stood watching the horrible weather.

Finally she drew herself up tall. "Well," she said, "my Romeo certainly won't be flying in this."

"Do you think he's all right?" Randall couldn't help asking.

Mrs. Mick grabbed a towel. She mopped a rain puddle from the floor by the open window of her bedroom. "I certainly hope so, dumpling."

Then she shut the window.

After Mrs. Anderson had come with her umbrella for Max, Randall spent the afternoon reading. The summer program was called Reading: What A Treasure. Randall had meant to show Mrs. Mick his card, but decided not to since Romeo was gone. It was a picture of a parrot. He got to color in one marked-off section of the picture with each book he read. When he'd done all seven sections, he could take his card to the library and get a prize. Something that had to do with treasure, and pirates and their parrots, the librarian had said.

But now was not the time to show Mrs. Mick.

The sky kept on raining. The world outside was a wavy blur. They went to the closed window more than once to see if Romeo might have made it back and been waiting on the ledge. Even though Mrs. Mick didn't want him trying to fly home in the wind and rain and thunder and lightning.

He wasn't there.

And Romeo was still gone when Randall left that evening. He went to sleep hoping the rain would stop and that Mrs. Mick's favorite game show would work its magic again.

Chapter 8
Under Attack

The game show failed Randall.

In the morning Romeo was still missing. The storm had passed. It was good flying weather, and Mrs. Mick had her window open, but Romeo wasn't home.

Randall was glad it was a Checkmate Squad morning. Mrs. Mick was crabby, and Randall suspected she was afraid she'd never get Romeo back. And he didn't know how to help. She even said she'd made a big blunder letting Romeo out.

"Such a noodlehead I am," she said.

"You want me to stay here and search for Romeo?" Randall asked.

"No, no. You're the leader. You and Max.

The Checkmate Squad needs you. Go on now."

"Well, okay. But I'll keep on the lookout for him."

So Randall and Max ran to the park. They wanted to get all four tables for the club this time. Robins were singing, the sky was blue blue. Randall would feel great if it weren't for Romeo being lost. He slowed to a walk. Max raced on to the tables.

Could Romeo have flown this far? There were lots of trees in the park. Randall craned his neck, but couldn't spot Romeo. Do birds ever get hit by lightning? he wondered. He hoped Romeo knew how to take care of himself. Unlike the robins, that bird was used to living indoors.

Poor Romeo! Poor Mrs. Mick!

At least Birdman wasn't in the park, Randall saw. That cheered him up. He helped Max put a few pieces on each table, kind of like a reserved sign. But really, he didn't think many people played in the mornings. So he didn't feel like a cheat—like the people in BurgerMart who always set a kid at a table while they waited in line for their food, so that the ones who'd gotten their food had no free table to sit at. Unfair, Mom always said.

He and Max talked over who should play together, and before they knew it, Dylan, Walker, Tara, Caitlin, Jenna, and Rosie were there. Yes! Randall told himself. It wouldn't be much of a club if they didn't all come.

"I practiced with my mom yesterday," Dylan said. "She and I are the only ones in our family who play chess."

Randall liked how he sounded proud.

He collected the "reserve" pieces from the tables. Others started setting up their games.

There was a scuttle of pigeons, and Randall was sure he knew who was coming down the path. Tall, gray, moving deliberately. Birdman.

Randall decided to give him the Gordo treatment—ignore him. He turned back to his board.

"Oh, my gosh! See that big bird he's got!" Walker said.

"Look at that!" said Tara.

Romeo! Randall immediately thought. He whipped around to see.

"Ohh, isn't it beauuutiful," moaned Jenna.

It was beautiful, Randall had to agree. But the bird Birdman carried was all white with a topknot. It was not Romeo. Randall blew out a breath. He didn't want to fight Birdman for Mrs. Mick's parrot. But he would if he had to.

Dylan went right up to Birdman. "Can I touch it?" He reached toward the man's shoulder, where the bird now sat.

"Eh, eh!" Birdman said. "Don't be pushy."

"What is it?" Dylan asked.

"Cockatoo, young man." Then he ran a finger gently down the bird's feathers. "It's my cockatoo, Elvira."

Suddenly Caitlin cried, "Oh, brother! Randall! There aren't chessmen for all the tables. Who messed up?"

Randall frowned. Huh? He had four

tables, but only enough chess sets for three! How had he let this happen?

Birdman pulled his velvet bag from the pocket of his baggy shorts. "For a game, I might be willing to share my pieces."

What? Randall scratched his head. He didn't want . . . This wasn't the way the Checkmate Squad was supposed to be. Not with an old man. Not with Birdman!

"Well, Randall?" Caitlin said. "What do we do?"

He looked at Max, who glanced at Bird-man. Much of the club was still oohing and ahhing over Elvira. He looked back at Randall and shrugged.

Randall felt trapped. "Okay," said Randall. "Uh, mister, you okay with playing with someone you have to teach?"

Birdman ambled over, sat down, and removed his chessmen one by one from the bag. Elvira stuck to his shoulder, hardly moving a feather. "I would have to teach anyone here."

Randall guessed that was true. But did he have to say it?

"I'll play him," said a small voice.

Randall wondered who had said that. Rosie came up to him.

"I play my grampa all the time," she said.

Randall figured Birdman would wipe out any of them in a few moves. Rosie was so tiny. And this was the first time he'd really heard her voice. But she sat right down, looking sure of herself. She might be okay.

"Thanks, Rosie," Max and Randall both said.

"Does your bird play?" she asked Bird-man softly.

For once, he almost smiled. "Elvira enjoys watching a good game of chess," he answered.

Now there was one extra club member, but Caitlin offered to watch. "That way I'll see what everyone does," she said.

Randall agreed, and everyone got down to playing.

"I remember bishops move diagonally, but can they move forward *and* back-ward? I think I forgot," Randall heard Jenna say.

Walker, who Randall was helping this time, said loudly, "Both ways." Then to Ran-dall, "That's right, isn't it?"

Randall smiled inside and out. His shoul-ders relaxed. "Yep, you got it." He hoped others remembered things as well as Walker did.

He made the first move. Walker moved his own pawn. Randall began to plan his strategy.

Then there was a change in the air—a heaviness—and a popping and slipping and scuffing sound. Randall stiffened. He knew Gordo had arrived.

Randall told himself, Ignore him, ignore him. But Gordo was hard to ignore.

In another moment Gordo was leaning on the table, taking everything in like a big, greedy sponge. He breathed through his mouth and popped his gum every minute, so Randall couldn't concentrate.

"Ha, ha, ha!" he cackled when Walker captured one of Randall's knights.

Randall glowered at him. "I meant that to happen," he said, then captured Walker's rook that had taken his knight. "A much more powerful piece to get off the board," Randall said.

"Oh, rats!" Walker said. "I forgot."

"Ahhh," Gordo said, as if he really understood. He popped his gum.

A little later Gordo was at Tara's table. Randall heard him loudly say, "Jenna, that's a stupid move."

"Huh?" she said.

"Wait. You'll see," Gordo said smugly.

"Ohhh," Jenna said when Tara took her piece.

"Ha! Told ya," said Gordo.

"You're not in the Checkmate Squad, Gordo," said Tara. "You're just here to cause trouble, like usual."

"Oh, what do *you* know?" Gordo said.

But Randall noticed he kept his mouth shut after that.

Rosie and Birdman didn't play anyone else all hour. They knew enough strategy to keep the game a real contest, and took a lot of time. Rosie swung her legs back and forth. Birdman petted Elvira. They each thought and thought.

Chapter 9
Captured!

After Randall's game with Walker, there was still time for a match with Caitlin. Now he had her king in check. Patiently he waited for her next move.

Rosie stood by watching because Birdman had just left. Randall asked, "Why did he go, Rosie? Sore loser?"

Rosie smiled at that. "No, he won. This time. He said he had to get Elvira back home."

Caitlin moved a piece, and Randall followed. "Checkmate," he said to Caitlin. "But you know how to keep that from happening next time . . . maybe?"

"Probably," Caitlin said. "I'm getting it."

"You made some good moves," Randall told her.

Then Rosie said, "She was sad."

"Huh?" said Randall. "The cockatoo was sad?"

"Yes. The parrot she's in love with flew away again, so she was sad."

Randall felt like he'd been jabbed. "In *love*?" he asked. "With a parrot? Birdman told you that?"

Rosie nodded. "He says when he leaves a window open, this parrot comes to visit. He stayed all night last night—'cause of the storm."

"Ohmygosh!" Randall leaped out of his seat. His heart was doing flips. How many loose parrots could there be?

"He left a window open this morning. In case the parrot decided to come back," Rosie said.

Birdman *must* be talking about Romeo. He had to find out. Now.

Right then the other old man, Harold, strolled up to the group. "Here you all are again. But where's my partner? Am I too late to play?"

Gordo bounced over. "I'll play you," he practically shouted.

Randall's eyes widened. Could anything worse happen? Besides, he *had* to get going. "Uh, our time's about up. Look, here comes Jenna's mother now. And there aren't any pieces for that table." He didn't like what he heard coming out of his own mouth, but it was better than telling Gordo, Go away, we don't want you. "I bet you don't know how to play, anyway." Randall glanced around to see if Birdman was still in sight.

"So? Half the kids here don't," Gordo said. "I know a lot more than you think, buddy."

Randall squirmed. Gordo was right. But this couldn't be! He swooped up his chess pieces. "Max!"

"What?"

"We gotta go. I think Birdman had Romeo last night. We have to follow him."

"Wow! Just a sec. We've got another play," Max said.

"Can't wait. Finish and catch up. See everybody next Tuesday." Randall took off. He cut across the grass. He saw Birdman about to cross the street, leaving the park. Good, he hadn't lost him.

Birdman walked fairly fast for an old guy. He seemed to have more spring in his step today. Randall slipped along, keeping close to buildings. He didn't want Birdman to see him. He just needed to know where the man lived so if Romeo left Mrs. Mick's again, Randall could get him back.

Birdman must have let Romeo out this morning—if what he told Rosie was to be believed—but what if he tried to keep Romeo for his Elvira so she would be happy? What if he tried to *steal* Mrs. Mick's parrot? Randall wouldn't put it past the old grump.

It wasn't long before Randall realized Birdman was retracing almost the same route *he* always took home.

Nooo!

Randall hid behind a mailbox. He peeked around. Birdman entered the courtyard to the apartment complex. He walked right past Randall and Max's beech tree. He turned the corner where Romeo had flown yesterday.

Then Max ran puffing up to Randall's hiding place. "Birdman lives *here*?" he squeaked.

Randall nodded with his finger to his lips. Then he motioned Max to follow him. He darted down the walk. Sneaked around the corner. Spied the man with the white bird step into the building.

They didn't dare follow him. What if he saw them? What if he still had Romeo and was so mean he actually hid Romeo from them? Or used that line about finders keepers?

"Look up," Randall said. "See if you find any open windows."

Max and Randall both scanned the three rows of windows. They both cried, "There!" But they each pointed to a different window, on different floors of the building.

"Count!" Max said.

"Third floor, first window, right side," Randall answered.

"Second floor, second window, left side," said Max.

"Come on," Randall said, and they raced back to Mrs. Mick's.

"Mrs. Mick, Mrs. Mick!" they shouted, flinging open her door. "Is Romeo here?"

"He is home, yes! You weren't gone ten minutes before he came back, strutting like a peacock—so proud of himself, the little rascal. He's given me a dozen Love ya, gorgeouses."

"That's because he's got a girlfriend!" Randall said.

Mrs. Mick huffed. "Well, he is my dear Romeo, but I am certainly not his girlfriend."

"Right," said Max. "Not you."

"A cockatoo!" Randall explained.

Mrs. Mick gave a little cough. She sat down. "What in the whole wide universe of nonsense are you two saying?"

"Birdman—" Randall started. "Remember the man in the park who loves the birds?"

"And he plays chess with us," said Max.

"He lives *here,* in building number four. He's the one Romeo goes to when he flies out the window," Randall finished.

"We were afraid he might still have your parrot, Mrs. Mick," said Max.

Randall explained, "Elvira—that's his cockatoo—is in love with Romeo."

"Well, you can stop worrying. No one is getting Romeo, in love or not. I'll keep the windows closed when he is out of his cage."

"But look Mrs. Mick . . ." said Randall, pointing.

The cage was empty. Randall could see through the open door, and Mrs. Mick's bedroom window was halfway up.

"Awww! What a noodlehead!" she cried.

Chapter 10
Who's in Check?

After finding that Romeo was nowhere in the apartment, the three of them marched over to the building Max and Randall had seen Birdman enter. It was three stories tall with a center entrance, just like Max's building and Randall's, too, so they could figure out which apartment numbers belonged to the open windows.

Now they stood at the door of the second floor, second window, left-side apartment.

"You ring the doorbell, Mrs. Mick," said Randall.

"No. You, please," she said. "I'm so upset, I might break the thing."

Randall rang, and chewed his lip.

They heard footsteps. The door was opened. A young woman holding a baby said, "May I help you?"

Randall blinked. This didn't look promising. "Uh, excuse us, do you have a cockatoo?"

"Do I—? A what? Is that a dog?" she asked.

"Not a dog, a bird," Max said.

"You're kidding, right? I've got two-month-old twins. What would I do with a bird?" She wasn't unfriendly. She just seemed tired.

"Thank you, anyway," said Mrs. Mick.

"Sorry to bother you," said Randall.

"On to the third floor, first window, right side," said Max.

Randall didn't hesitate to ring the doorbell this time. Just thinking about Birdman got him riled up. The way he was so unhelpful but still barged into the club. The way he was planning to steal Romeo. Boy! Better watch out for me, mister, Randall thought.

But then there he was. So tall. Feathery eyebrows drawn down. Icy gray eyes staring at Randall from his doorway. It stopped Randall for a moment. Mrs. Mick and Max were silent, too.

"Well, well," Birdman said, slowly taking in the three of them. "Didn't realize you boys knew where I lived."

"You've got Mrs. Mick's parrot!" Randall blurted out, getting his nerve back.

"Love ya, gorgeous!" They all heard it, loud and definite. It came from inside the apartment.

At that, Mrs. Mick stomped past Birdman, her ponytail swishing, chin out.

"Now wait just one min—" Birdman started.

"Romeo, Romeo!" Mrs. Mick cried. She turned on a heel. Shaking a finger at Birdman, she demanded, "All right, where is my parrot?"

"Oh, don't be so dramatic, woman. He's safe and sound in the next room. If he hasn't already flown out again."

"Dramatic! Well!" Mrs. Mick bristled.

Randall didn't think he should interrupt. Maybe Mrs. Mick could handle this. But he still had his eye on Birdman.

It was a standoff for a minute, then Birdman seemed to decide he'd met his match in Mrs. Mick. In a quieter tone he said, "I am sorry to have caused you alarm. It isn't

that I invited your fine bird here, and I have wanted to find out who he belongs to."

"Wellll," Mrs. Mick said. "I've been careless, a tad, I admit."

Birdman nodded toward the boys. "I am acquainted with these young men. Randall and Max, I believe." Then he held out his hand to Mrs. Mick. "I'm Jacob Winn."

"Madeline Mickovitch," she said, shaking his hand. "I must look a mess. I was so worried about my bird." She tucked a stray wisp of hair behind her ear.

Randall shot a glance at Max. He looked as puzzled as Randall felt. Seemed like Mrs. Mick was letting Birdman off the hook.

"Come on into the living room," Birdman said. "Your parrot has my Elvira in a tizzy, I'm afraid. She is happiest when he is here."

"Well, he is quite a bird," said Mrs. Mick. Then she saw Romeo and Elvira.

"Ohh!" Mrs. Mick said. "Did you ever see two more beautiful birds?"

Mr. Winn smiled. "No, I don't believe I have. And I'm a great fan of birds."

Mrs. Mick's own smile grew a few watts brighter at that.

"Elvira makes a fuss when he leaves," said Mr. Winn. "But I knew he had to belong to someone, so I never shut him in, you see. Except last night. He would have been in danger in that wild storm."

Randall thought Birdman . . . uh . . . Mr. Winn's voice had changed. He sounded nice! And suddenly he didn't look so gray.

Mrs. Mick said, "I won't be letting Romeo fly away free again. Next time he might not find such a safe open window."

"Wise, of course," said Mr. Winn. "Elvira will get used to being alone once again." His face seemed to droop when he said that.

Maybe—Randall was thinking—maybe Mr. Winn wasn't the ogre he had thought he was. Maybe he felt as lonely as Elvira was about to.

Then Mrs. Mick was saying something about arranging times for the lovebirds to be together. "Why don't you bring Elvira over to my place tomorrow, say ten o'clock?"

"Well, I . . . I . . . ," Birdman stuttered. "I don't get out much—except to the park to feed the pigeons."

"Oh, please, so Romeo and Elvira won't be lonely? And you and I can share some tea?"

Mr. Winn swallowed. "Fine. Yes, that will be good for the birds."

But the way Birdman and Mrs. Mick were looking at each other, Randall had a suspicion it might be good for more than just Romeo and Elvira.

When they left soon after, Mr. Winn said, "And I'll see you boys at the chess tables?"

Randall said, "Bye," without really answering that question.

Later, at home, Randall helped his mother clear the dishes. Supper had been his favorite, spaghetti and meatballs with Mom's great tomato sauce. But it hadn't taken his mind off his problems.

"You're quiet tonight," Mom said. "What are you stewing about?"

Randall knew he should have told her sooner about all that had happened today. But he'd been sure he wouldn't be able to eat if he started talking about Gordo. *Or* Mr. Winn. He handed Mom a plate to load into the dishwasher.

"Weird day, that's all," he said. His stomach rumbled and rolled. Maybe he shouldn't have eaten at all.

"I'd like to hear about your weird day," she said, studying him.

Randall put his head in his hands. "It's Gordo. And Birdman."

"What?" She touched his shoulder lightly.

Randall suddenly was talking as fast as he could. "Birdman had Mrs. Mick's parrot, but we got him back and now they are friends, and his name is really Mr. Winn, and he wants to keep playing chess with us. And so does Gordo!" Randall felt a burp coming. He definitely shouldn't have eaten that eighth meatball.

"Oh, you have had a day." She pulled him into her for a hug. "Would that be so bad?" she asked. "For them to be in the club?"

And that's when the big burp blasted out of Randall's mouth.

Mom pushed him back. "Do I get an apology for that?" she asked, but she was chuckling.

Randall couldn't laugh. "I'm sorry. I'm going to my room. I've got thinking to do," he said, scurrying off.

It wasn't till later when Randall was in his pajamas and brushing his teeth after talking a long while on the phone with Max—it wasn't till then that Randall finally made his decision.

He fell asleep easily, without a single rumble from his stomach.

Chapter 11
Endgame

Three weeks later—that was six chess club meetings later—Randall stood in the community meeting room of the library. Because that's where the Checkmate Squad met now. And because Randall was being interviewed by a *Rushport News* reporter.

"You will make a great human-interest story. It isn't often that young people today share activities with older folks of the community," the reporter had said.

Now she held a notepad and pen ready. "So your name is Randall?"

"Yes, ma'am."

"Is that one *l* or two?"

"Huh? Oh, two. Two *l*'s." It both excited him and made him nervous to be asked questions by a real reporter.

"You are the one who started this chess club, is that right?"

Randall poked Max's arm. "My friend Max and I started the Checkmate Squad. I needed a project for the summer. And Max is a good partner."

Max grinned, making his ears go up like usual.

"How did you come up with the plan to have seniors join with your school friends?"

"Well, it just sort of happened," Randall said. "At first it wasn't that way. It was kids from our third grade class, plus Rosie. Then Mr. Winn and Harold came, then Romeo flew in Mr. Winn's window and fell in love with Elvira, then . . . "

The reporter had stopped making notes. She looked at Randall oddly. "This is seeming like more of a story than I had imagined, " she said.

"Uh, what I mean is . . . is . . . ," Randall said.

Tara came up. "Spit it out, man."

Randall tried again. "Once Mr. Winn wanted to join, and Gordo wanted to join," Randall said, glancing at Gordo, who was playing a game with Harold, shouting only once in a while, "it seemed a good idea to move into this nice big room in the library and to invite enough old people to equal the kids. I thought it might be too complicated at first. But the library was glad to have us. And Mr. Winn got the rest of the old—I mean, seniors."

The reporter glanced at Mr. Winn. "It's good to see Jacob Winn taking part again. He was mayor of Rushport for six years, you know."

Randall's jaw dropped. He hadn't known, of course.

"Oh, yes. Always had a hand in making our town a good place to live. But, off the record, when his wife died a few years ago, he almost gave up on life. I don't think he was meant to be alone, like he has been. So sad and lonely, he became quite a curmudgeon, I hear."

"I don't think he is lonely anymore," Randall said, looking at Mrs. Mick.

Mrs. Mick turned from her game with Caitlin and waved at Randall. Even she had decided playing chess would be a good thing—she needed to spread her *own* wings. Of course, it also gave her more chances to spend time with Mr. Winn, she had told Randall.

Randall scanned the room. Walker played with Birdman, Dylan with Harold's brother Elmer, Rosie with a lady named Pearl, Jenna with a senior named Jack. And Tara had just finished a game with Bob. "That's the Checkmate Squad!" he said proudly.

"Well, you've done something nice for the community." The reporter held her hand in the air like she was writing words she could see. "New boy in town draws together old and young to share the great game of chess." She smiled at Randall. "I think you'll like the article I'm going to write."

Randall felt himself blush. "Thank you, ma'am," he said.

"My last question is, how would you say your project turned out?"

Randall knew the answer. "It isn't the chess club we planned. It's better."

Tara gave him a big thumbs-up, and Max and Randall high-fived. Yay, Checkmate Squad! Randall thought. And yay, Rushport, his new hometown!

On their way back to her apartment, Mrs. Mick said she and Mr. Winn had a date tonight. "Yes, dumpling, Jacob is taking me dancing!"

Love ya, gorgeous! thought Randall.

RandalL's Guide To Chess

HEY RANDALL! TEACH US
HOW TO PLAY CHESS!

RANDALL: Sure. Chess is played on a board that looks like this.

With pieces that look like this.

Every game starts with pieces set this way.

THAT'S COOL. HOW DO YOU MOVE?

RANDALL: Tell them, Max.

MAX: First, you have to know the ways each piece can move. Here's how it goes—

ROOKS   Move up or down or side to side in a straight line. They cannot move diagonally. Rooks can move as many squares as you want as long as they are not blocked.

KNIGHTS   Move in any direction: forward, backward, or to the sides. They always move in an L-shape: two squares in a straight line and then one to the side. AND they can jump!

BISHOPS Move diagonally backward or forward as many squares at a time as you want.

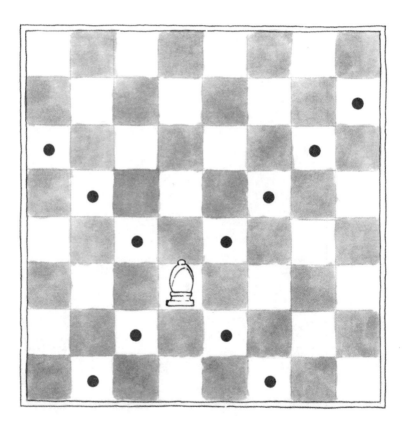

QUEEN   Moves in any one direction for any
         number of squares.

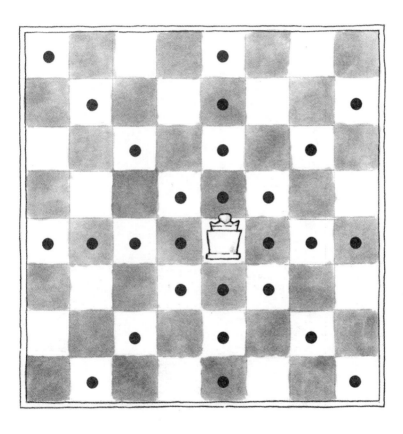

KING   Moves in any direction but only
one square at a time.

PAWNS   Move forward in a straight line one square at a time. Their first move is special because they can move forward two spaces. AND they move one square diagonally when they are capturing a piece. There are eight pawns for each side.

YIKES! I'M LOST ALREADY.

RANDALL: Don't worry. The more you play, the more you remember.

ROSIE: I like the queen. The king is important, but the queen is the most powerful.

CAITLIN: The goal is to get your opponent's king trapped so you could capture him in your next move.

JENNA: I know, I know! That's called "in check."

GORDO: Yeah, obliterate the guy!

MAX: We should put *you* in check.

TARA: Checkmate! That's when you can't save your king from check, and I win!

RANDALL: You got it.

BUT HOW DO YOU PLAY?

MAX: Play with people who know how and help you learn.

RANDALL: And read up on chess in a library book.

BIRDMAN: Practice!

RANDALL: You'll learn lots of strategies—how to think ahead to stop moves your opponent might be planning.

RANDALL and MAX: Have fun!

Author's Note:

The two resources I used are listed below:

Castor, Harriet. *Starting Chess*. London: Usborne Publishing Ltd., 1995.

Eade, James. *Chess for Dummies*. New York: Hungry Minds, Inc., 1999.